Dear Parents,

Welcome to the Scholastic Reader series. We have taken over 80 years of experience with teachers, parents, and children and put it into a program that is designed to match your child's interests and skills.

Level 1—Short sentences and stories made up of words kids can sound out using their phonics skills and words that are important to remember.

Level 2—Longer sentences and stories with words kids need to know and new "big" words that they will want to know.

Level 3—From sentences to paragraphs to longer stories, these books have large "chunks" of texts and are made up of a rich vocabulary.

Level 4—First chapter books with more words and fewer pictures.

It is important that children learn to read well enough to succeed in school and beyond. Here are ideas for reading this book with your child:

- Look at the book together. Encourage your child to read the title and make a prediction about the story.
- Read the book together. Encourage your child to sound out words when appropriate. When your child struggles, you can help by providing the word.
- Encourage your child to retell the story. This is a great way to check for comprehension.
- Have your child take the fluency test on the last page to check progress.

Scholastic Readers are designed to support your child's efforts to learn how to read at every age and every stage. Enjoy helping your child learn to read and love to read.

—**Francie Alexander**
Chief Education Officer
Scholastic Education

Copyright © 1997 by Nancy Hall, Inc.
Fluency activities copyright © 2003 Scholastic Inc.

Library of Congress Cataloging-in-Publication Data is available.

ISBN 0-439-59416-2

10 9 8 7 6 5   09 10

Printed in the U.S.A.   23
First printing, February 1997

I AM NOT A DINOSAUR

by Mary Packard

Illustrated by Nate Evans

Scholastic Reader — Level 1

SCHOLASTIC INC.

New York Toronto London Auckland Sydney
Mexico City New Delhi Hong Kong Buenos Aires

I am not a dinosaur.

I don't have horns.

My legs are short.

My feet are small—

Not like a dinosaur at all!

I wish I had a special tail,

A longer neck,

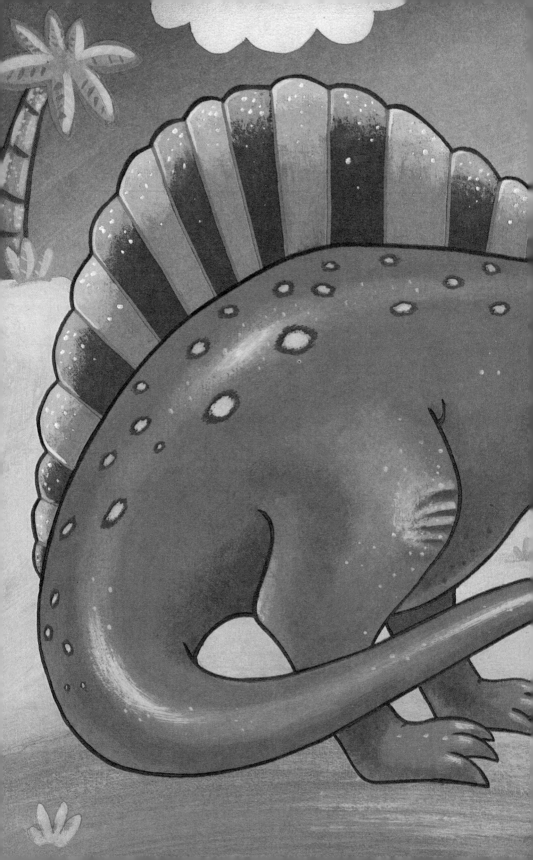

A special sail.

Although I do not have a crest,

Fly Away

The animal in this story is not a dinosaur.
It is a **Rhamphorynchus**!
It has wings and can fly, and is actually a bird.

If you had wings like the **Rhamphorynchus**,
where would *you* fly?

Dinosaur Search

Find five dinosaurs hidden in this picture.

D Is for Dinosaurs

Point to the pictures of the words that begin with the letter D.

Rhyming Words

In each row, point to the object that rhymes with
the word on the left.

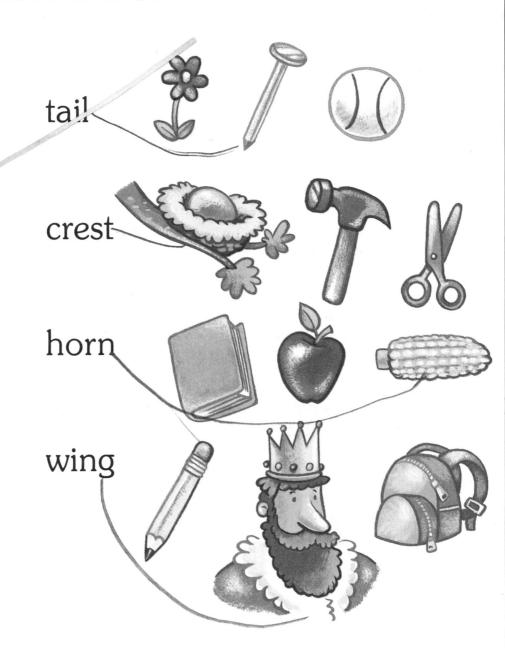

tail

crest

horn

wing

Words and Meanings

Some words have more than one meaning.

A **horn** is a part of an animal,
and a **horn** is also a musical instrument.

The first sentence in each pair gives one meaning
for a word. Read the second sentence and point to
the picture at the bottom of the page that shows
another meaning of that word.

A **ring** is a sound that a telephone makes.
A **ring** is also a

A **ball** is a fancy party where people dance.
A **ball** is also a

A **pen** is a place where pigs are kept.
A **pen** is also a

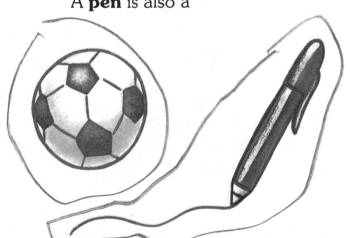

Animals

Some animals have body parts that make them different from other animals.

Match each animal on the left to its special body part on the right.

bull   fin

fish   wing

bird   shell

turtle   horn

Answers

(Fly Away)

Answers will vary.

(Dinosaur Search)

The hidden dinosaurs
are circled here ------------>

(D is for Dinosaurs)

These begin with D:

(Rhyming Words)

tail	crest	horn	wing

(Words and Meanings)

A ring is also a

A ball is also a

A pen is also a

(Animals)

bull —————— fin
fish ————×——— wing
bird ————×——— shell
turtle ——————— horn